HALLOWED OBLIVION

other books by katherine silva

<u>The Wild Oblivion</u>
The Wild Dark
The Wild Fall
Hallowed Oblivion
Lost Oblivion
Orchards
Dan & Andy's Scary-Oke Holiday

<u>Deadlands</u>
Undead Folk
Dead Folk
Nothingland

<u>The Monstrum Chronicles</u>
Vox: Book 1
Aequitas: Book 2
Memento Mori: Book 3
Acquolina: A Short Story

The Collection
Night Time, Dotted Line

HALLOWED OBLIVION

BY

KATHERINE SILVA

Strange Wilds Press

5 P.M.

HALLOWEEN

Gina opened the app on her phone and hit record.

"What's up, bitches? My friends and I are here at Shimmering Rock in the heart of the White Mountains and we're summoning ghosts!"

She panned the camera around a small dirt clearing. In the background, three other people waved as they dropped their gear and stretched. Overhead, the dusky sky ignited with yellow and pink stripes. Fiery leaves scattered down around the teens with the gusting wind.

Gina laughed as she turned to point the camera at a gargantuan stone monolith behind her.

"Shimmering Rock is the site of sixteen deaths and over forty disappearances in the last ten years. Tonight, the night before Halloween, we're going to connect with those lost spirits and hopefully hear where we can find the bodies they left beh—"

Something smacked her shoulder and Gina growled before hitting the large button on her phone to stop recording. She picked up the still-wobbling acorn from its spot on the ground. "Seriously, Art? I've had to redo this video, like, six times already."

"When are you going to help us start setting up instead of taking photos of yourself?"

Gina glared. "We're not going to get the views unless I get this intro right. You *do* want us to get views, yeah?"

"Maybe not as much as I'd like to set up camp and take a quick nap. We've been hiking all day." He pushed a hand through his greasy red hair and rolled his eyes at her.

"Shut the fuck up, Art," Nicki muttered. "This needs to be on point. Otherwise, ThoseSpookyGuys won't see our video and we won't get the collab opportunity."

"You know how many people are going to be doing this hashtag challenge?" David piped up as he unzipped the tent bag and started pulling stakes out. "Hundreds. Thousands. You've got maybe ten thousand followers at best, Gina. I think we should just eat some lunch and head back down."

"No fucking way," Gina said. "Just because you're afraid your churchy Nana is going to find out doesn't mean we're stopping."

"Does your Nana watch TikTok?" Art chuckled.

David sputtered. "N-no, you dumbass! But if we're not back by the time we said, someone's—"

Gina spun toward David. "No one is going to come looking for us, because you were supposed to call your mom and tell her we were staying out for one more night?"

When David didn't answer, Gina took a step toward him. "Right?"

He stared at the ground. "I couldn't get reception on my phone. I tried. I *really* tried!"

Rage pulsed through Gina, her temples throbbing with the new anger. "Are you kidding? David, why the fuck didn't you say anything?"

"So, what now?" Art interrupted. "Is she going to send forest rangers out to find us?"

"They don't even know we came here," Nicki said. "Because we didn't want David's grandmother to get upset about him messing with ghosts."

"Great," Gina muttered, sitting at one of the picnic tables nearby. "Just great."

Nicki approached and sat next to her. She bumped Gina's shoulder with her own. "Maybe this is a blessing in disguise. It does sound kind of nice. We could go down to that quaint little town, Card…Cardoff?"

"Cardend," she said.

"—Anyway, we could go rent a room at an inn, maybe send the boys out to find dinner and call David's mom…" Nicki gave her a wink. "Have some alone time."

Gina smirked. "As much as I'd love that, we have work to do. I've promised my fans—" she gave David a look, "—All twelve thousand of them, that we would be doing the challenge. I've got to do this to build my brand. If I want to succeed at this influencer thing, I need to stick to what I say."

Nicki sighed and kissed Gina's cheek. "Fine." She whirled around and headed back to Art and David. "Looks like we're out here for the night, gentlemen! You'd better try calling your mom, David."

David huffed while Art laughed.

"Little Haystack Mountain is about half a mile that way." Gina pointed. "You could get a signal there."

David pulled out his phone and tapped the screen. After a moment, he tapped again, "My phone's dead."

Ignoring him, Gina positioned her phone in front of her again and hit record once more. "Tonight, on Halloween, we're going to connect with those lost spirits and hopefully hear where we can find the bodies they left behind."

She picked up a nearby stick. "Next step: draw a giant pentagram. See you bitches later!"

Earlier

2 P.M.

Hank ignored the chatter on his radio as he tipped his coffee mug back to drain the dregs from it. Tonight, he'd enjoy a full night's sleep after the longest week of work.

Evie's spoon plinked into her empty bowl.

He gave her a side-eye.

His daughter licked her lips for the last smears of chocolate ice cream and looked up at him with her puppy-dog eyes. She grinned shyly.

His heart melted.

Anne, the owner of the diner, rubbed at a plate with a rag behind the counter. "I know that smile," the woman said, tucking a loose silver bang back behind her ear. "I think this little ghoul is going to fill her bucket with candy tonight."

Hank leaned over toward Evie. "Is that the plan, Eves? Candy-pocalypse?"

Evie nodded.

Both he and Anne let out soft laughs.

"Awful brave of you to take her out for sugar early in the day, Hank," Anne collected the empty ice cream bowl. "You're lucky if she doesn't start climbing the walls after tonight."

"Maybe. I think I owe her after last year though."

"She didn't get to go trick-or-treating?"

His thoughts darkened. "I took Melissa to rehab that day. It was bad and I probably shouldn't have waited so long. I didn't want Evie to see it. She had a sitter but I guess I picked a bad one. You know the Lacey girl? Pam, I think?"

Anne scoffed. "I know the one."

"When I got home, they were watching some, like, C or D rated horror film with a bunch of sex and serial killers." He gritted his teeth. "I had to explain a few things I wasn't ready to."

Anne laughed. "That bad, huh?"

Evie perked up. "Daddy said it was fake. No one really bleeds that way if someone cuts their—"

"You get the picture," Hank interrupted, looking at Evie. "Honey, why don't you go put the crayons back over on the shelf over there."

She slid down off her stool and scampered over to a red bookcase against the wall.

Hank turned back to Anne. "Anyway, it was a long night. Lots of nightmares; lots of asking where Mommy was... I don't want her to remember Halloween like that."

Cardend was a small town. Everyone knew someone who knew something and in his world, that meant they knew he and his wife, Melissa, had separated a little over a month ago due to her increasingly devastating opioid addiction. There was only so much he could do to hold on and support her. After years and years of standing by, watching as Melissa chose to endanger her life, chose the drugs over their daughter and him time and time again, he finally couldn't do it anymore. It was the hardest decision he'd ever had to make.

Evie climbed back up onto her stool. She leaned on the counter with her head on her crossed arms, staring at a saltshaker while she rapidly closed and opened alternating eyes. He'd shown her this trick only a few minutes ago when she'd devoured her ice cream and it still held her fascination.

He squinted. Had her hair grown another inch? It seemed like his daughter was changing in some little way every day and he was barely able to keep track of it. His job kept him up in the mountains and often away from Evie for several hours a day. Not tonight though.

Tonight, they were going to celebrate out on the town, putting into action Evie's crayon-sketched candy-collection map. They'd start with the grandiose Queen Annes up on Howlett Point Drive, meander down through the one-way cottages owned by the little old ladies who lived on Spearneck Avenue until they reached the town center.

There, they'd take full advantage of all the brick-and-mortar businesses handing out goodies. The general store usually passed out popcorn necklaces and Joanne at Cardend Hardware made magic wands from wooden dowels and sparkling tinsel. They'd stop into the local bakery where Chef Blake would be handing out his famous Dino Bars, named for the dinosaur-foot stencil he molded his chocolate chip blondie brownies in.

Newly outfitted, he and Evie would traipse down the main street where cars were prohibited from driving that evening and glimpse all the spooky festivities: silent films at the old movie theater, the costume contest over at the townhall, and the old mill museum that always put on a cheap if not satisfying slideshow of ghost stories in the White Mountains.

The doors would be festooned in black and orange crepe paper, windows hung with the silhouettes of skeletons and bats, the air perfumed by marshmallow sugariness and haunted with mock screams and laughter.

And then they'd go home, back to their cozy apartment on Lochlin Hill overlooking the river. The last few houses they'd hit would be that of their neighbors, who all had something special set aside for her: oatmeal cream pies, or fake vampire teeth. They'd settle in: Evie to take stock of her spoils and Hank to kick back in his armchair with a mug of tea and maybe a horror short story. He liked Poe. It had been too long since he'd read any of Poe.

The radio scratched on his hip again. Hank was pulled out of his reverie by what sounded like his name being spoken over the static. They weren't supposed to call him in tonight. He had pleaded for someone else to take his shift months ago so that Evie could have her magical night. Maybe someone just had a question? They couldn't find something and needed his help…

"Sounds like their hailing you, champ," someone said from down the bar. Hank glanced down toward an older man chewing on a club sandwich and eyeing his radio with a faint smirk.

Gerard Castle was one of Cardend's seasonal residents who owned a cabin on the Old Notch Road. He came for several weeks throughout the fall and stayed until the snow began to fly. Castle kept to himself during the day: fly-fishing, reading, and working on his small cabin. Though quiet, Castle was personable and was often ready with a wry, Dad joke that Hank had somehow never heard before.

"Why did a scarecrow will the Nobel Prize? Because he was outstanding in his field."

"What did one plate say to another? Dinner is on me."

There'd been many a night where they had played a game of pool at the local bar with beers in hand, sharing a few laughs.

Hank gave Castle a nod and looked to Anne. "Would you mind watching her while I take this call?"

Anne rounded the counter to sit with Evie at the barstool he'd vacated. "Tell me, little lady, what are your top five candies?"

Hank unholstered his walkie and stepped out the front door, the bell above jingling to signal his departure.

Main street was abustle. People sat outside Anne's enjoying coffee at their sidewalk tables. A strong breeze clutched at their bare necks and ungloved hands. Parents with costumed children tucked into shops to escape the wind; families emerged from the laundromat with baskets full of warm clothes. Two men on ladders set up strings of orange lights that spiraled down the lamp posts on each side of the street. Anticipation and excitement tinged the air.

Hank suddenly felt insecure about everything, like there was a fist scrunching onto his prospects.

Before he could speak into his radio, his phone rang. He recognized the number: one of his colleagues from the station. "Hello?"

"Hank, I've been trying to reach you. I need you to come in."

"Dan, I asked for this time off months ago."

"We've got a call in about a group of overdue hikers. A mother said her son went with a group of friends a few days ago and they were supposed to be back last night. She hasn't been able to get in touch with him."

"Any idea which tent site they were staying at?"

"They were supposed to be doing the Pemi loop. Guyot last night…maybe."

Hank frowned. "Seems like someone ought to have run across them then."

Cooper cleared his throat. "There's something else."

"What?"

"Mom doesn't think they were staying on the Pemi Loop."

"Why not?"

"Because of the Tik Tok trend."

Hank was silent.

"About seeking out local legends?"

"Can you please speak to me like I'm not seventeen, Dan?"

"It was in the fucking news, Hank. The new trend is about visiting sites of local ghost stories on Halloween. Apparently, the teen, David: his sister found a video about it on one of his friend's social media pages. David was in the video."

"Any new videos since yesterday?"

"None."

A gust of air swooped down through Hank's hair and slinked along his neck. He popped the collar on his jacket. "Plenty of ghosts in the graveyard. Why not go there?"

"Do you know how many people have died in The White Mountains?" Cooper asked.

"Lots."

"So, you tell me: what happens when a bunch of teenagers go out into these woods searching for ghosts with not an experienced hiker among them?"

Hank breathed in through his nose and held it for a few seconds before letting it go. "You've got search and rescue?"

Cooper hummed.

"You've got MRS?"

"Yeah."

"You've got Walter and Clara and Donovan from AMC."

"I need you, Hank."

"Why? Why do you need me, too?"

"Because I asked you."

Disbelief and anger ignited together and within moments, burned out. Helplessness took over. Kids were lost: dumb kids following some dumb trend on the dumb internet. But they were someone's daughters; someone's sons... Just because he wanted to give his daughter a deserved Halloween night didn't mean he could shrug them off as someone else's problem.

What's worse was he was about eighty-five percent sure search and rescue would find them all gathered off one of the major trails, drinking and playing around with a Ouija board. The parents would get sent the requisite bill and the kids told that, because of them, government resources had been wasted and yada yada yada…

And who would really be impacted by this?

He glanced over his shoulder at the window of the diner where Evie sat talking to Anne.

Damn it.

"Hank?" Cooper asked.

Fucking damn it.

Hank sighed. "Where do you need me?"

"Head up to Franconia Notch. I need you to check the Ridge between Lafayette and Lincoln. It's the only place I don't have eyes."

"I'll get my gear assembled and radio you when I'm out there." Hank ended the call and stared at the phone, trying to keep the tide of curses in check. He couldn't do it.

"FUCK!"

Two older women coming up the sidewalk flinched.

"Sorry. I'm *so* sorry."

They turned around and went back the way they came.

"Doesn't sound like that was a good call," someone said.

Gerard Castle joined him at the curb and zipped up his Carhartt canvas jacket. In spite of his ability to get along with nearly everyone, Castle seemed as though he were modeled after a creature from another world. Standing beside Hank, he towered over the ranger, his build bonier and lanky. There were many times when they'd shared a beer that Hank felt a loneliness to Castle, as though his solitude was because he missed whatever alien planet he'd left behind.

Hank sighed. "Lost hikers. I have to go out and help find them."

Castle's eyes rounded behind his rectangular glasses. "I'm sorry. I know how you were looking forward to tonight."

"I'm not sure how I'm going to break it to Evie." The thought alone made Hank's cheeks tingle and his eyes sting. It was too last minute to find a babysitter. Angel, her usual sitter, was going out to a party and he would never subject her to Pam again. That meant only one person he could ask, the one person he'd had to fight with in order to get Evie for Halloween: Melissa.

Castle patted Hank's shoulder. "She's a tough cookie, Hank. I think she'll understand."

"But she'll be disappointed."

Castle nodded. "What else can you do?"

The question was rhetorical but Hank found himself scrambling through empty options nonetheless. He was probably going to be out all night unless search and rescue or the other rangers caught a break. There was no one who could stay with her but her own mom.

"Hey," Castle said. He was staring at Hank expectantly.

"Sorry. I'm all over the place right now. What did you say?"

"I asked if they're looking for volunteers. The more people out there, the faster they might find those kids."

"We've got everyone from MRS and SAR along with volunteers from AMC. They'll cover different points of the Pemi Loop starting from different trail locations. Probably could use more though."

Pemigewasset had a strong summer staff, plenty of volunteers, and enough caretakers out maintaining huts so that if someone did vanish, they were usually found fairly quickly. Now that the season was at its tail end, they'd lost most of their help. Two of their longtime rangers had retired in August and few with qualifications had even answered the advertisement for help wanted.

"Where are they having you look?" Castle asked.

"Franconia Ridge." Hank was already making a gear list in his head and was trying to remember where he'd left his second set of thermals.

"Tell you what: I'll go back to the cabin and grab my gear. I'll meet you over at the Notch and we can start out together."

Hank frowned. "I appreciate the offer, Mr. Castle, but—"

"But what? They can't expect you to go out there on your own, can they?"

"I'm sure he'll have me meet up with some of the other rescuers once I get up there."

"Yeah, but that's, like, what? A five, six-hour hike? Come on. I'll keep you company and give you a second set of eyes."

He didn't need company, at least, that's what Hank wanted to tell him. This was a rescue operation and it didn't behoove Hank to have to watch out for not only a set of lost teenagers but also an older man who would probably slow his progress. "Listen, really, it's not—"

Castle clapped him on the back. "Good, it's settled. I'll meet you at Franconia Notch in an hour." He had crossed the street before Hank could voice his disapproval, climbed into his white pickup truck, and even waved before rumbling into traffic.

Whatever shits Hank had left to give were deflated with the departure of Castle's truck.

3:00 P.M.

They didn't listen to any music as Hank drove Evie to Melissa's. He'd put on her favorite music, The Eagles, which was one of the only actual cassettes he had left that would play in the old Jeep, but she'd told him to turn it off.

"I'm sad and I don't want to be interrupted," she pouted as she stared out her window.

"You know this is a part of my job, Eves," he answered. "I was hoping this wasn't going to happen. But I don't get to decide. I have to help."

She wiped her eyes dramatically and let out a tiny sob. "Why didn't those people just stay home and go out trick-or-treating?" A small tear rolled down her chin and hung there.

He looked back up to the road, a stone of hurt in his stomach. He turned onto Melissa's street. "I don't know, honey. But you know what? You and your mom are going to have fun, okay?"

The words felt like a lie. He didn't know that. He didn't know what Melissa had planned last minute. He doubted she would take Evie out trick-or-treating. Melissa didn't go out much these days anyway. People talked. Now that she was trying to curb her habit, there were people in town better left alone, even on Halloween.

Melissa's house was last on the street: a white raised ranch house with a gold sedan parked in the driveway. The garden was glazed in fallen leaves and bursting with weeds; the front walk moss-covered and neglected. He pulled the Jeep up to the curb and turned off the engine.

Evie cried harder. "It's not fair!"

"Come here." He unbuckled her seatbelt and pulled her over into his lap where she let herself be dragged, her little shoulders hitching with each snuffle.

They sat there for a minute and Hank kissed her hair. The sobbing quieted and eventually ceased.

Evie rubbed her nose. "When are you coming back?"

Hank checked the clock on his phone: it was ten after three. He needed to be over at Franconia Notch in a half an hour to meet Castle, even if he didn't want the latter there in the first place.

He doubted Cooper would keep them out in the woods for longer than the night. Another shift of people would likely take over as soon as the sun came up. Still, that would be the whole night gone.

Instead of saying this, he shrugged. "I'm not sure."

She mumbled something.

"What, honey?"

"I don't want you to get lost, too."

The sentiment was new and it immediately emptied his lungs. She'd never said something like this before. "I'm going to be fine. I'm going into the woods prepared. I have my first aid kit, warm clothes, a GPS, and all the other bells and whistles they give me. That's the difference and I'll be coming back to you, okay?"

Evie stared before finally nodding.

When Hank looked up to the house, Melissa stood on the stoop outside the front door. She'd cut her hair short and wasn't wearing makeup like she usually did. It made her seem frailer and two-dimensional, almost like a cardboard silhouette more than a human being.

He opened his door and got out, bringing Evie with him. Her packed purple bag swung onto the ground as he planted her feet on the lawn. He bent down to pick it up and handed it to her. "Soon as I'm off the mountain, I'll come and get you, okay?"

She kissed his cheek though the effort felt half-hearted and rushed across the lawn to Melissa before he had time to return the token of affection.

He made eye contact with Melissa as she bent down to hug Evie. The sadness that spanned between them filled Hank with guilt.

He climbed back in the Jeep, started it up, and drove away.

The sun had vanished behind grey clouds as Hank turned his Jeep into the Bridle Path Falling Waters Trailhead parking lot. He was nervous. If they had bad weather up there, this would make it harder to find the stranded teens.

The parking lot was still full at this point in the afternoon, even this late in the season. The Old Bridle Path was a popular trail with the locals and the Lafayette Campground was just down the road. A couple were exiting the trail as he parked the Jeep, their leashed Golden Retriever wagging its tail happily as they bantered.

Hank noticed Castle's old pick-up truck a few spots away and parked as close as he could. Castle put up the tailgate on his truck bed and slung a small daypack on his shoulder.

Hank's own pack was probably twenty to thirty liters larger than Castle's and teemed with carabiners, ropes and accessory straps. He'd packed his climbing gear, emergency camp food, a stove and fuel, doubled up his first aid supplies, brought back-up headlamps, maps, and a knife. Granted, he wasn't as fully outfitted as search and rescue, but he was ready for most of the usual eventualities that befell inexperienced hikers on these trails. Most important was the GPS. If he did find the missing teens, he could send a message straight to Cooper that would help search and rescue pin-point their location.

Castle waved and Hank got out of his truck. After collecting their things, they gathered at the bottom of the trailhead.

Hank eyed the small backpack. "Are you sure you want to do this?"

The older man gave him a wide smile. "Why? Are you afraid I'll break a hip?"

"How old are you?"

"Ah, what are you ageist now?"

Hank grinned. "Not to sound like a jerk, but maybe I am afraid you *will* break a hip, Mr. Castle."

"Gerry. And I just turned seventy a month ago."

Hank blinked. "That's…a big one."

Castle snickered. "You know, before I retired and moved to New England with my family, I was a field biologist. I studied liverworts, horworts, and—"

Hank narrowed his gaze. "—Moss."

Castle pointed a finger at him. "You got it."

"Not to sound like a jerk about this either but you seem like the type."

"The point I was trying to make was that I've hiked all over the states, Hank. Even here in The White Mountains. In fact, I'm a part of a current bryology study with New Hampshire as part of an environmental monitoring program. I come out here to collect samples and take notes and send all that data back to the University of New England."

Hank scoffed. "And here I thought retirement was all about *not* doing the work you devoted your whole life to."

"Well, I guess if you love it enough, it becomes more than work. Maybe you'll discover that in twenty to thirty years." He winked.

"Maybe." Hank took a deep breath. "I'm worried you're not prepared for what you're getting into."

Castle's smile thinned.

"We're ascending four-thousand feet before nightfall on some difficult terrain. Once we reach, Lafayette, we are going to keep hiking. In the event that the weather turns, we'll have to hole up at one of the local shelters. Since we'll have already passed Greenleaf Hut, that means pushing onto the Liberty Springs campsite and doing it in sleet or snow. We're going to be out here most of the night. Temperatures will hit as low as the twenties." Hank shook his head. "I can't bring you out here if you don't understand the risks."

Castle's eyes kind of glazed over, as if he was lost in a memory.

Hank felt more alone than ever with the prospect that he had rightfully scared his would-be partner off.

But Castle's features brightened and he said, "Then, we'd better not waste any more time. Let's go."

They walked into the woods.

5:30 P.M.

Old Bridle Trail meandered through the forest on a well-worn path before reaching a steep ascent that required more time and effort to climb. As the trail blazes lessened and the rocks got larger and more challenging to climb, Hank knew they'd be hiking in the dark before they could reach Greenleaf Hut.

Hank had hiked Old Bridle more times than he could count and had averaged a time of about three hours with good conditions and enough light to see where he was going. While he was fit, the rocky terrain was still tricky in places to find a safe route that both of them could travel.

Castle took longer to find his footing. Hank waited ahead on the trail more than a few times while his companion clambered around on the rocks below, finding an easier way up.

Settling the headlamp onto his forehead, Hank let its intense white light pierce the surrounding dusk. The sun was a whisker of red light on the horizon. They hadn't seen a single person on their ascent in over an hour and each person they'd asked hadn't seen hide nor hair of the missing kids.

This was the off-season and the Greenleaf Hut would be closed as they didn't have a caretaker for it nor was it heated. While it was more than likely they wouldn't find the teens at Greenleaf, there was a chance the kids could have broken in if they were desperate enough.

So far, Hank and Castle's hike hadn't provided many places for kids to go off trail in order to conjure up spiritual harbingers.

More than anything, Hank just wanted to get to the hut, so they could radio in and see if anyone had found any signs of them yet. Communication was spotty in the mountains. He wasn't sure his phone could even get reception at this point.

A scrabbling of rock below brought Hank's attention back to the trail behind him. Castle emerged over the edge of a rock, his form swelling and shrinking with each puff. By the time he made it to Hank, he was gulping down air like a distressed swimmer.

"We're almost there," Hank assured. "Once we get to the hut, I can get you set up to stay there while I continue on to Lincoln."

Castle sucked in a breath, his own headlamp blinding as he stood up tall. "You're that eager to get rid of me, eh?"

"It's nothing personal, Mr. Castle."

"Gerry."

A high-pitched screech echoed up from the wind somewhere from their left. Both men craned their heads toward it.

"Coyote," Castle said.

"Yeah. It's far off though."

They continued on. Hank pulled the load-lifting straps on his pack to take some of the weight off his lower back. They had another hour or so before they'd see the cabin.

"Suppose it's likely those kids could have run into some wildlife out here?" Castle said. He reached for a handhold, his long fingers edging around the curve of a rock by Hank's foot.

"Anything is possible," Hank said.

"Any chance you've got bear spray on you?"

"Yeah, but we'll be lucky if we see a black bear right now. They're probably hibernating. Besides, they're non-aggressive. Just make yourself look big and intimidating and they'll head off in another direction."

"Good, good." Castle hummed to himself. "Anything else out here besides the weather we should be on the lookout for?"

"Ghosts and goblins, I guess." Hank forced himself to smile despite a bluster of cold air careening down on him from above.

The two of them continued up, the landscape morphing as the trees were left behind, the rocks slipping into their shadowy coats in the nighttime, the shrubs bristling against the wind. Air pinched and nipped at their clothes as it swirled about them.

The trail plateaued. As they meandered along its dusty path, Hank noticed the ragged outline of

Greenleaf Hut against the gloam of green on the horizon. "There it is."

They crossed the distance to the hut much quicker with the promise of getting out of the razor wind. Hank opened the lockbox next to the door to reveal the hut key. After unlocking the hut, they bumbled inside with their gear and shut out the cold and the dark.

Hank flicked on a light.

Greenleaf opened into a wide room with several picnic-styled wooden tables on the left, a kitchen and tiny shop to the right. They explored the rooms, flashlights swaying back and forth through the dark corridors and empty spaces. The building branched off into washrooms and bedrooms with multiple bunks in them. During the summer and autumn seasons, travelers could reserve space there and stay for the night, even expect a freshly cooked breakfast for themselves in the morning. On the eve of November, the room was freezing. An eerie hum from the lights pervaded the space.

After they finished looking around, Castle shrugged off his pack and sat down at one of the picnic tables in the main room. "Doesn't look like anything is out of place here."

"Nope. No windows broken, none of the cabinets opened…" Hank scratched his head. Where were these kids at?

He looked back at Castle.

The older man was winded. As soon as he noticed Hank staring, determination slid back into his face. "Gimme a few minutes and then we can hit the Ridge."

"Take a few more. I'm going to call Cooper and see if he's got any updates for us."

Castle nodded and unzipped his pack.

Hank meandered into the back office where an emergency radio sat. Slumping into the chair there, he flipped on the desk lamp, tuned the radio to the right frequency and spoke into the mic. "Cooper, this is Feld. We've reached Greenleaf. Do you have any updates?"

The radio crackled. Hank's eyes were drawn to his own faded reflection looking back at him from the glass in the window before him.

Outside, the blue darkness conquered everything. Only the stark black mountains struck out against the sky; cold and without apparent life.

"Feld, this is Cooper. We've just heard back from a couple of the other parents. Apparently, the teens destination was near Shimmering Rock. Sorry I couldn't get that information to you sooner. It could have knocked some time off your hike."

Hank scanned the map pinned to a cork board nearby that showed a detailed topography of the Ridge. It included everything from Garfield Mountain over to the Flume. Shimmering Rock was a popular tourist attraction located a quarter mile past Little Haystack Mountain at the other end of the Franconia Ridge loop.

Taking the Falling Waters trail would have shaved at least an hour off their time though that hike would have been more challenging for Castle to ascend.

Shimmering Rock was down a small side trail that split off of the Ridge Trail. Unlike the more well-known Shining Rock, located off of Falling Waters, Shimmering was a tower-like monument of granite that jutted out from the mountainside. It was as though someone had taken a brick and stuck it into the mountain at a forty-five-degree angle. Sometimes, the way the light hit it caused it to appear like it was made of black glass. Despite Hank's many trips up along the ridgeline, he had never been to Shimmering Rock.

"Feld? Feld, how long until you can get over there?"

Hank took a deep breath. "It's going to take me at least another hour or so. I have a volunteer with me."

Cooper didn't respond. Hank pictured his boss surrounded by groups of anxious people, fielding calls left and right and trying to coordinate everyone's movements on a large map spread over their table at the station.

"How long is it going to take for you to send someone else up to meet us when we get there?" he added.

"I've got six from MRS heading up to Franconia now. The wind is too bad to send up a chopper. It will take them a couple hours. You'll be on your own for a little bit."

Hank hummed.

"If those kids are there, you activate that emergency beacon. If not, sit tight."

"Over and out."

Stiff and unconfident, Hank returned to the main dining room.

Castle was finishing a second protein bar. As Hank walked in, he crinkled the wrappers up and stuffed them down into his bag. "What's the scoop?"

Hank filled him in, taking a moment to drink from his own water bottle.

"Shimmering Rock, huh?" Castle whistled. "I've heard of that place."

"Popular with the tourists," Hank said. "Popular engagement spot, too. Guess something about a giant sparkling rock makes people want to commit to a life-long bond with each other."

Castle threaded his fingers. "Says a man who is currently disillusioned with his marriage."

Hank's throat tightened with the comment. It wasn't wrong but it still hurt to have it be called out. "I have good reason."

"You do." Castle's tone was earnest; his eyes apologetic.

Hank changed the conversation. "Why had you heard of Shimmering Rock?"

"It's an ecological dead zone; one of the only places in the White Mountain National Forest where no moss grows. It should by all accounts and yet, it doesn't."

Hank sighed. "Great. That bodes well."

The two men sat silently for a few minutes, preparing themselves for the return to the hike.

"Why did you want to come out here with me?" Hank asked.

Castle stared at the floor, nodding to himself. "I like it if I can help out. Plus, I didn't have stellar plans for the evening. Thought about catching that silent film at the theater but wasn't sure."

"You'd rather abuse yourself hiking all night versus enjoy a movie?"

"I'm retired. I have plenty of time for movies. Besides, I've got to stay active. The yoga helps but this is better. Really gets the blood moving."

Hank sat at one of the neighboring tables. "I get the feeling it's not just that."

Castle shrugged. "Go on."

"There was something… You had a look when I tried to get you not to come."

Castle closed his eyes and remained that way for a while.

Hank began to wonder if he'd drifted off to sleep when Castle said, "Because of David."

"Who?"

"My son, David. He was killed in a car collision up here in the Whites. In fact, it was on the very road I live off of. A car came over the line and they think he swerved his bike to avoid them. It had just rained. They found the bike at the bottom of a steep ravine off the side of the road. He was about…twenty feet further into the woods."

Hank's throat burned as he listened. "I'm sorry."

Castle's voice broke. "The impact had broken most of the bones in his legs and his left arm was missing." He inhaled sharply. "He was a good kid. I was lucky. He was getting his doctorate in public policy of all things. I remember talking to him just before he left to come up here and he told me to pick up some of his favorite beer. He was an IPA guy. I never liked the stuff."

"That's what you order every time I've seen you at the bar."

"It's grown on me." He stood up, donning an extra set of mittens. "We're losing time. We should go."

Hank cut the lights and they set out once more on the ridge.

8:00 P.M.

Hiking Franconia Ridge was like crawling along like the spine of some enormous beast. Its jagged rocks made the exposed trail treacherous.

After summiting Mount Lafayette and then Lincoln, Hank and Castle headed toward Little Haystack Mountain with heads down, watching their footing and fighting the gusts that barreled into them.

The wind was a constant soft roar in Hank's ears. He thought about Evie the whole time as he plunged his trekking poles into the earth with each step. By now, if all had gone according to plan, they would have been returning home for bed-time. He wondered what Melissa had done for Evie that night. Had they played games? Watched spooky films? What did they do for dinner? Was Melissa's house even decorated inside for Halloween?

"Hey!"

Hank stopped and looked back at Castle.

He pointed at the trail ahead of them.

All at once, Hank's self-calm broke and his lungs collapsed.

A body lie face-down in the middle of the trail.

Scrambling over the rocks, Hank threw himself down in front of it. As he scanned the head down along the torso and the arms for injuries, he stopped at the waistline. Ribbons of fabric and flesh draped over the rocks and ended in a spray of blood where the legs should have been. He turned the body over with hesitation. The corpse's face came into view. Hank's throat closed as he reeled over onto his back.

The teenage boy's eyes had rolled up into his head to reveal the whites though the sockets were stretched so wide, they seemed to swallow each one in their vastness. His mouth stiffened into a horrifying gape, lips pulled back and split in places to fully expose his teeth and gums. The skin seemed an unusual pale, even for the environment: the color of glistening metal under frost.

"Breathe, Hank," Castle said over and over, his voice now directly overhead, hand clamped on his shoulder. The sound of his voice washed in and out with the wind.

The hood on the boy's sweater flapped around wildly in the gusts.

Finally, air plunged down into his gut and Hank gulped it down. "Holy shit! Holy shit!"

Castle scuttled over to inspect the body and jerked away, coughing into his fist so hard that his whole body spasmed.

Hank fumbled with the GPS on his belt and marked the location, his eyes barely leaving the body.

Castle crawled back to Hank. "He doesn't have a backpack. And no jacket."

"Probably ran from the campsite."

"A bear tracked him all the way out here? Onto the exposed ridge?"

Hank didn't say anything. There was no way to determine when this had happened other than that it probably wasn't during the day when people were still actively hiking on the ridge. It had to have been after dark, perhaps no less than an hour ago. There was a chance others were still alive. It also meant the chance of an enraged animal close by.

Gathering themselves, the men pressed on, leaving the boy's body behind.

"You said black bears were non-aggressive," Castle said, close behind.

"Well, so am I but if you do something to piss me off, guess what? That changes."

"Tell me you've got that can of bear spray ready."

"Usually, you'll hear the bear before you see it. We'll have a warning."

Castle scoffed. "Are you kidding me? With all this shit blowing around, you expect us to hear a bear snorting?"

A scream pierced the darkness, riding on the gusts and floating up into the heavens.

The hair on Hank's arms prickled. "Let's go."

Little Haystack Mountain loomed ahead, the last open rocky expanse on the ridgeline. Ahead of them, the Franconia Ridge Trail resumed down into the whisking trees while to their right, the Falling Waters Trail dropped down the mountain back toward Franconia Notch.

For several moments, Hank's cowardice bucked inside. He wanted to wait for the Search and Rescue team to meet them before they continued. More people might be a safer way to continue forward, especially if there was a bear waiting for them at Shimmering Rock.

But that scream…

Those kids needed him now. He couldn't wait.

He also recognized there hadn't been another scream after the first.

"Fuck, fuck, fuck…" Hank chanted to himself as they continued ahead into the forest.

All at once, the trees enshrouded like a closing mouth and the brutal wind diminished. Branches quaked overhead, their last clinging leaves like teeth chittering all around them.

Hank pulled his neck gaiter up over his nose, trying to keep his breath from obscuring his vision. It was darker here in the woods and his headlamp, though powerful, barely cut through it, like shining a flashlight through crude oil.

"Which direction did that scream come from?" Castle whispered.

"It's hard to tell. The sounds bounce around in here like crazy."

They made it a few more steps, their boots crunching on loose twigs and crispy leaves.

In the gloom ahead, a shriek made Hank's head swim with terror. "That's Shimmering Rock, off to the—"

Another cry lifted from their far right.

"They're separated," Castle said, a quiver in his voice.

Hank whirled to him. "I'll go to Shimmering Rock. You check out the other one."

"I've got nothing to defend myself!"

"There's only one bear. Two screams. It can't be in both places at once."

"Bears can run, Hank, and I don't know if you noticed but I'm not much of a runner anymore."

Squatting, Hank slung his pack off and unzipped the brain of the bag, yanking out the bear spray. He shoved it into Castle's arms. "Not that it'll do much if a bear is running *at* you."

Then, he ran, leaving Castle behind.

This was stupid. *He* was stupid for rushing into danger like this. He should have sent the GPS signal back there when he'd had a moment to think. But he was triggered by the scream, by the idea that someone might have been actively dying while he stood there and did nothing.

Hank clambered down some natural rock steps and grabbed at the trunk of an ash tree to keep his footing on the moss. The Shimmering Rock marker appeared out of the haziness before him along with pained whimpering. Hank barely braced himself before he darted down the short path toward the rock.

9 P.M.

Castle snuck along the trail. Hank had vanished almost within moments of him taking off. If Castle stopped moving, he could still hear his footfalls echoing far off in the dark.

He hadn't heard anything after the initial screams and as he clutched the can of bear spray in his hand, he wondered if he was ready to potentially encounter one of the three-hundred-pound beasts in the night like this.

The leaves rustled a foot in front of him and Castle jolted back, holding the can out defensively.

A red squirrel twittered angrily at him before darting across the trail into the brush.

"Little shit," he grumbled.

Something slammed into him, nearly knocking him off his feet.

Castle spun toward the shivering, shrieking girl collapsed on the ground at his feet. "Whoa, whoa! It's okay!"

She leapt up and latched onto him. Her fingers clung to the folds in his jacket, her nails dug into his arms. "Please, help me! Help me, help me, don't let it get me…"

Instinct took over Castle's mind, an instinct that he'd driven around time and time again whenever he needed to be a voice of reason, whenever his wife lost her strength. It made him feel in control, despite being in a situation where he was far from it.

"Easy, easy. Slow down."

Dirt smudged the girl's face and hands. She was barefoot. Muddy pajama pants and a BU sweatshirt hung off her quavering figure.

He tried to look her in the eye. "What's your name?"

"G-G-Gina…"

"Gina, I need you to tell me where your friends are, okay?"

Her face scrunched up and the sobbing started again. "I d-don't know where Art is! He ran off. Nicki is…she… And David… He was back at camp."

Castle's heart stilled. The last boy had the same name as his son. There were a lot of kids named David. It shouldn't have hit him with such force. But it did and even as Castle thought to himself, *Don't let it affect you. You're okay*, all of his muscles steadily tightened.

"Where's the bear? Do you know?"

Finally, she made eye contact with him. "It's not a bear."

"What?"

A low grumble bristled over the shrubs nearby.

"God! No!" Gina tore out of Castle's grip and flung herself down the other side of the trail.

Castle swung his flashlight toward the growl. The light was swallowed up entirely. Only blackness looked back.

He turned back toward the fleeing girl. "Hey!" he yelled, his voice booming across the forest. "Come back!"

Castle ran after her.

Hank descended a steep hillside, scurrying in places so his boots wouldn't slip out from underneath him. Despite the cold, this area of the forest was slick and strangely warmer than the rest of their hike had been. Distantly, he wasn't as worried about the temperature as much as he was about finding the owner of that scream he'd heard.

The trail evened out and as Hank reached stone once more, he took in the sight of Shimmering Rock for the first time.

The clearing allowed the moon to blaze in unimpeded and ignite the monolith in its glow. Standing nearly forty feet tall, the rock erupted out of the mountain at a strange angle, its naturally flat faces sliced as if by stone carvers. The nearest side shone a distorted image of the forest back at him, filmed over by the black color of the rock. Over the years, people had climbed up it to take their photos at its zenith, leaving eroded hand and foot holes corkscrewing up it.

The Shimmering Rock rest area wasn't meant to be a campsite, but these teens had set up their pair of two-person tents, had stenciled what appeared to be a large pentagram in the dirt just beneath the rock and had even lit candles. Those candles were tossed about the half-smudged out pentagram now, the tents left in disarray with the poles bent and jutting up into the air at odd angles. Splashes of blood shone black in the light.

Hank approached the first downed tent and pulled at the rainfly to detangle it from the frame. A pair of eyes stared up at him from a rumpled sleeping bag. Hank nearly dropped the material in surprise.

The eyes didn't change.

Peeling the rainfly away further revealed the rest of the teen's face and where the rest of her body should have been. Her eyes were wide and white, as if Hank had accidentally scared her, too, and her mouth slackened. Like the body they'd come across on the ridge, what was left of the girl was an unnatural shade of steel grey.

Deep under the wreckage of the tent was another lump. He continued lifting the tent.

"Shhhh…"

The hiss made him kneel down.

A teenage boy lay on his stomach, eyes pleading as he stared at Hank. He was blubbering to himself, his face coated in sweat, tears and dirt.

Hank extended a hand. "You can come out. The bear is gone."

The boy swung his head wildly. "No… It'll hear me. It'll find me."

"Give me your hand."

The boy shuddered before he reached out.

The tent exploded in movement. Hank scrambled back on hands and knees as the entire structure was dragged into the shrubs, the boy screaming incoherently along with it. The rustling faded into the trees until the squeal was abruptly silenced.

Hank's limbs were paralyzed. His thoughts raced as he heard the end of the scream over and over in his head.

The brush in front of him shook.

Hank crawled toward the shadows of the forest, toward where he'd first descended into the campsite. As he slipped into the darkness, a shape burst from the thicket.

Curled on the cold earth, vulnerable and unarmed, Hank quickly shut off his headlamp as he watched the creature's approach.

The boy's body slammed lifelessly into the moonlight in front of the Shimmering Rock. He was facing away from Hank. for the briefest moment, Hank was thankful he couldn't see the last look of horror he imagined the kid had.

The boy's fingers moved.

Hank tensed.

Fuck.

He was *still* alive.

The shadows stirred and gathered together into a vast frame, smooth and alien. Powerful legs slipped into the moonshine, bringing the dark void with them. Sculpted from the night, the creature's long snout poked into the light, maw open to reveal fangs the color of moss-sheltered white quartz. The worst were its eyes. What Hank had glimpsed as golden embers for a brief moment before were now the palest shining of white, as though the moon were reflected in each eye.

One moment, it stood over the teen and the next, there was utter chaos.

Enormous talons shredded the boy's calves like knives slicing through tender meat. A vortex of shadow and dust swirled up, partially obscuring Hank's vision of the events. The unearthly wail anchored his gaze toward the disturbing tableau, his own insides twisting with every hitched breath and high-pitched howl.

The wind abated.

Feathery strands of something like moonshine streamed in currents from the teen's body into the creatures waiting mouth. The boy's eyes expanded, larger and larger until the skin around each socket ripped. The flesh on his forehead, cheeks, and chin was stretched up and back over the crown of his skull, leaving what was once his face empty and featureless. His fingers curled in the air as if trying to hold onto something invisible.

The darkness recessed, leaving the body in the blurred moonlight amidst a new kind of silence.

Tears raced down Hank's face. He rubbed his eyes, his lips trembling as he quietly sniffled. He didn't want to move. He didn't realize he wasn't breathing until he made himself inhale. Fuzzy spots filled his vision as he tried to calm himself down.

After a few more moments, his breaths had evened out. There was still one more teen up on this mountain unaccounted for. He also had no idea where Castle was. They needed to get out of here before that thing found them all.

Waiting in the silence for a few more moments, Hank quietly climbed back up the route he'd taken out of the Shimmering Rock rest area. His eyes never left the contorted corpse.

Once he'd shimmied up the embankment, Hank dropped to his knees in the leaves and shakily grabbed hold of his GPS. He fired off the emergency signal. Nothing happened. Unable to read the display, he fumbled to get his headlamp turned back on.

`Lost Satellite Signal`

Hank tried it again. The same message popped up.

He'd used the GPS on the ridge not that long ago. How could he lose the signal to the satellite? This was why the station upgraded to these GPS devices…

Hank weighed his options. He could follow the trail back to Little Haystack Mountain where he would hopefully run into the other Search and Rescue team and warn them about what was ahead.

Hank took a step but stopped himself short. He couldn't leave Castle behind.

The blame bubbled up inside of him as he thought about what the older man had told him back at Greenleaf Hut. He'd come out here because it made him feel as if he was still relevant after his son's death and it was Hank's responsibility to make sure that nothing bad happened to him. What was he going to do when Castle's wife asked what happened to her husband?

No. He couldn't let personal feelings get in the way of what was the most logical option. He needed to find help. For all he knew, Castle was already dead. He needed to meet up with Search and Rescue.

Hank looked up to continue forward.

Darkness blocked the path. The beast was closer than it had been in the clearing and Hank realized it was twice as large as he'd first thought, its head at the same level as his shoulders. Its snarl reminded Hank of roiling water from a deadly current.

Hank took an unconscious step back and his heel caught on a rock. As he fell, the creature sprung. Fur grazed his face and a claw carved into his bicep before he thudded against the ground.

The creature had missed landing on him, launching over him into the trees on his right.

Hank picked himself up and ran in the first direction he could: deeper into the woods.

9:30 P.M.

Castle caught his breath as he listened to the inhuman scream ricochet through the night. It was the worst sound he'd ever heard and he wanted nothing more than to tear his ears off than to keep listening to it.

It abruptly stopped and he sunk onto his knees on the forest floor, exhaling rapidly.

He'd lost sight of Gina when they hit a flat section of the mountain. He listened and heard nothing but the wind in the trees. An owl called somewhere far off, startling him.

Shit... he thought as he plunged his hands into his coat pockets, giving them a little relief from the cold. The worst thing to befall a hiker was becoming too cold and exhausted out here to hike. The second worst was to lose the trail.

Sliding his compass from his pack, Castle inspected it beneath the harsh light of his headlamp. The dial sat at dead south.

Strange. He was pretty sure he was facing west, judging from where the moonlight was coming. He tapped the glass face. The needle stayed put.

The compass was old but he'd used it only a few days ago while checking on moss samples in the woods and it had been fine then…

Castle tucked the compass away. He had a general idea of where the trail was behind him anyway. Cautiously, he patrolled a bit further until the trees opened up. A steep decline dropped off into a craggy expanse below. Tiny evergreens peered up at him like stiff fur on the mountainside.

The girl couldn't have gone any further. There was a chance she had turned and fled further into the woods to the south but he'd have seen and heard her.

She was hiding.

Castle started back through the woods toward the trail and cleared his throat.

"Gina! My name is Gerry. I'm part of a search and rescue party that's come up here to find you and your friends. If we're going to get out of here, we need to find the trail and head back toward Falling Waters."

He waited.

Nothing moved.

"I know you're scared. I'm not going to leave you. As long as we stick together, we'll be alright."

Something moved out of the corner of his vision.

Castle turned toward the nearest tree.

Gina cowered against the trunk, half-shrouded by the tree's shadow. As soon as she saw him looking at her, she curled up into a tighter ball. Her crying intensified.

Castle knelt down next to her. "It's okay. Here: take my hand." He reached out.

She didn't move.

He inched closer. "Come on. It's okay."

Gradually, she unfurled like a plant feeling the first rays of sun after the night. Her icy fingers slipped into his.

He helped her up. Unzipping his outer layer, Castle quickly swept his coat over the girl's shoulders and helped guide her arms through each sleeve. He pulled the hood up over her head. "Are you hurt anywhere?"

Her voice was faint. "My ankle. I tripped."

"Do you think you can walk on it?"

She didn't answer, but he could tell she was weighing the response.

Where was Hank when he needed him? The answer gnawed at Castle. He thought about the horrific scream from earlier and it took everything he had not to imagine Hank torn to pieces in the same way his own son had been.

Castle swallowed hard. "I wish I could carry you but I don't think I can. My back isn't exactly what it used to be."

Digging into his pack, he found his ancient first aid kit and unrolled an ACE bandage from it. He instructed her to lift up her pajama pant leg and once she had, he set to work wrapping up her ankle. Just as he finished, a low wind whistled through the trees. At least, that's what Castle assumed it was. Then he heard it again and it stretched on for longer than the first before escalating into an eerie high pitch.

Gina's shivering became a full-body tremor.

"We're gonna move kind of fast, Gina. Are you ready?" he asked.

She nodded.

They limped through the underbrush. Castle let her lean on him for support. Each step felt like it took three times longer than it should have. By the time they reached the hillside, Gina was whining in pain and Castle's shoulder throbbed with the added pressure of her weight.

"This is going to be the tough part," he told her, gritting his teeth. "It'll hurt, but it's important we get to the trailhead. I'm going to stay behind you, okay? I won't let you fall. You'll have to use your hands to help steady yourself."

Gina forged ahead without another word, first trying to limp up the side of the hill without touching her injured foot down. She wobbled and Castle quickly caught her before she crashed back down into him. "Good effort. Try getting a bit lower and really rely on that other leg."

This time, the going was easier for her. She scaled the hill in less time than he was expecting and he kept close to her in case whatever creature had been chasing her suddenly made its appearance.

Back on the trail, Castle sighed in relief. "Falling Waters is this way."

From the darkness behind them, there was a faint voice. "Dad."

The memory of it was like a knife in Castle's gut, twisting ever so slightly. He turned around and frowned.

Someone was standing on the trail about ten feet away from them. Castle squinted, trying to make out features in the dark. He looked at Gina. "Is that one of your friends?"

She looked back and forth from the trail to him before she quietly answered, "There's no one there."

Castle blinked. Something about the way the figure was standing made his mouth dry. Were they wearing a motorcycle jacket? It looked the same as the one David had—

A shout burst out of the forest somewhere in the woods. Castle recognized the voice immediately.

"Hank…"

When he returned his gaze to the end of the trail, he noticed the figure had vanished.

Pointing toward Little Haystack, Castle said, "Go, Gina. Search and rescue are coming up the Falling Waters trail. They'll find you. Tell them we need help!"

"Wait," she peeped, snagging his hand as he started to go. "Don't! Don't go!"

"Run, Gina!" Castle instructed as he started further down the trail toward where he'd heard Hank's cry.

❧

Hank didn't look back, knowing any hesitation meant death. The trail sloped ahead, turning rootier and more dangerous. These were not the trails he'd spent his whole career hiking. This one was more twisted, the trees closer and blacker than he remembered, the ground more treacherous. Watching his footing was crucial. If he tripped, he might never get back up again.

The sound of claws in dirt behind him spurred him on, labored breaths growing closer and closer behind him. His heart was a steel drum, his mouth and throat tasted like iron. Every breath he took razed his lungs.

The growling deepened.

Hank threw himself down and to the side of where the trail descended.

The creature blundered down the rocks past where he'd rolled.

Doubling back, Hank swung around a small tree as he ran back toward Shimmering Rock. His headlamp bobbed back and forth, highlighting strange spots of the trail: a bush here, a tree branch or rock there…

Talons scraped against stone behind him.

He was out of time. There was no way he could outrun this thing on the trail, let alone on a flat road. He was going to tire but first, it was going to catch up to him and do whatever it had done to those poor kids. He needed a way to kill it and quick.

A snort of air at his back made Hank yell out in terror. He pushed himself harder. He wasn't going to make it. It was just too—

Sudden weight slammed into him. Hank careened down the hillside into the foliage. Tumbling, Hank protected his face with his arms before his body crashed into a partially-downed tree.

Side lancing in pain, Hank struggled to stand. He inhaled and his lungs fought back. Stumbling through the weeds and into a clearing, Hank recognized the familiar sight of Shimmering Rock and the teen's grotesque body strewn atop the pentagram.

His breath puffed into the air in short bursts. *This is how I'm going to die.*

The brush trembled behind him.

Hank sprinted toward the rock, frenzied and desperate. Cupping his fingers into the worn handholds, he launched himself up against the slanted part of Shimmering Rock. His boots scrabbled against the smooth face to climb up.

The dark shape swept into the clearing as though smoke were pouring into an open room.

Hank hauled himself up, his foot connecting with the first notch in the rock. Moments later, the other foot did the same. Hand after hand, foot after foot, he climbed around the curve until he reached the top of the slanted portion.

Claws bit into the stone near his foot with a horrible crunch.

Hank inched further up the rock toward its highest point, using more hand and foot holes to guide his way. He was at least ten to fifteen feet up already.

Below, the monster paced below the rock, its icy white gaze trained on his every move.

Keep going! He pushed himself on.

Then came a worse sound: multiple claws ticking on stone. The creature leapt the distance from ground to rock easily, landing several feet behind him.

Hank swore and kept going. Soon enough, he could see the night through the evergreens more clearly, feel the bite of the bitter wind as it clipped at him through his jacket. The pentagram and the body below were small, dizzying reminders of the fate that awaited him should he fall or be caught.

Using the flat of his palms to help pull himself up against the angled top of Shimmering Rock, Hank reached its highest point. Forty feet up in the air, the gusts blasted his exposed body, the cold cutting against his cheeks and freezing the sweat on his brow.

He'd thought nothing that creature's size could get up here and now he'd backed himself onto a precipice. Either this thing was going to maul him and tear him to pieces at the top of Shimmering Rock or he'd fall and break most of the bones in his body.

Hank turned as the black form approached him. Its claws shrieked against the stone as its stare bore into him; eyes like white, shining discs. Its jaw opened to reveal a long vacuous gullet and pin-thin fangs that glistened in pearlescent shades beneath the moon. The fur around its chest and legs was stained with dried blood.

Evie. I'm sorry.

It leapt at him; claws extended.

Hank threw himself to the side of the rock, pitching down over the edge. Even as his stomach dropped and panic seized him, Hank scraped and clung to whatever he could, his elbows and fingers raked against stone until he stopped moving. His lower half dangled over the cliff's edge.

The creature landed in the spot where he'd been and slid, careening over the tip of the rock. It howled as it vanished from sight. Moments later, he heard its body crumple against the earth.

Trying to dig is elbows into the rock for better purchase, Hank gasped as he slid backwards. Crying out in fear, he fell.

Two hands snatched Hank's hand. Hank stopped short, blindly gripping whoever had saved him. When he looked up, he saw Castle, his face engraved in resolve.

Taking his other hand, Castle heaved Hank back up onto the rock. Grunting and groaning, the two fell across the slanted surface in exhaustion.

"Thanks," Hank said breathlessly.

"You can thank my yoga instructor," Castle answered, lying flat on his back.

Hank crawled to the zenith of the rock and peered over its edge. The creature was gone. Even weirder, so was the body of the teenage boy. Faint traces of the drawn pentagram were left behind in a scuffle of claws against dirt and a trail of blood that scraped off in the direction of the woods to the south.

Sagging onto the stone, Hank took his first few relieved breaths of air before looking back at Castle. "How did you get up here?"

Castle frowned at him. "Same way you did: staircase on the other side."

Hank stiffened. He looked over at the other side of the rock. Sure enough, a wooden staircase had been built for visitors to climb up to the top of Shimmering Rock. Hank fell back against the stone with a chuckle. "Damn it."

Moments later, a flashlight beam swept into the clearing followed by someone shouting, "Hank! That you up there?"

Hank rolled his head to the side.

A team of people entered the area, radios chattering and lights swimming in the darkness all around. One of the Search and Rescue officers stood near the ruined tents, taking in the damage. Another was standing near the base of the rock, shining a light up at him. After the beam fell away, Hank recognized him as one of their long-time search and rescue volunteers, Andy.

"I'm here, Andy," he called back.

Andy swept his flashlight beam over toward the pentagram. "What the fuck happened out here?"

Hank looked expectantly at Castle, hoping the latter had a better explanation than he did. They stared at each other blankly.

"I don't rightly know," Hank eventually said. "But I want to get down off this damn rock."

NOVEMBER 1ST

7 A.M.

It was hours before Hank and Castle were back down off the mountain.

The search and rescue teams had found Gina nearly collapsed at Little Haystack Mountain ranting about a monster killing her friends and proclaiming Hank and Castle were in danger. Going to the spot where Hank had marked on his GPS revealed no body, nor did they find the other two bodies of Gina's friends at the campsite or in the surrounding woods. The blood they collected eventually came back as a match to her friend, David. Though the case was still open until they managed to recover the bodies, it was suspected that the other three teens were killed by a rabid bear.

As the sun's first rays stained the sky, Hank gave his account of the events in the Old Bridle Trail parking lot while sitting in the back of an ambulance. The paramedic applied a bandage to the scrape on his arm and waggled a flashlight in front of his face.

Castle approached the back of the ambulance, favoring his left foot. He glanced at the paramedic. "What's the word?"

"Mild shock, possible concussion. We'll know more once we get him down to the hospital."

Hank frowned. "I need to get Evie."

The paramedic shook his head. "You really should go to the ER to get checked out."

"I'll take him," Castle said, pointing to his truck.

The two of them traipsed across the dusty parking lot to Castle's beat pick-up truck and climbed inside, hinges squeaking as they closed the doors. As they rumbled back out onto Route 93 and headed south, they sat in silence, both staring at the road straight ahead.

"Thanks, Gerry," Hank said hesitantly.

"Don't mention it," the older said with a small smile.

"Did you ever…" Hank searched for the words. "…Did you ever see what that thing was?"

Castle shook his head.

Hank stared down at his boots. "I feel like I imagined the whole fucking thing."

"You didn't." Castle changed gears. "But I don't think we'll ever understand what happened."

Hank nodded absently.

Puttering through town, Castle gunned the truck up around the main street, passed the little cottages toward Melissa's road where Hank directed him to park at the last house. The truck idled while Hank climbed out and followed the front walk up to the door.

After a few moments, it opened to Melissa in the same clothes as she had on yesterday. She took one look at Hank and reached out to hug him. He let her, lost in a past natural occurrence, even wrapped one arm around her in return. This was strange but it also felt okay, and okay was all he needed right now.

Evie appeared behind her. Relief settled over him like a warm current. He knelt down and wrapped her in a tight hug. "Hi, Eves. I told you I'd be back."

Castle parked his car along the side of the notch road and killed the engine. He was just a few miles from his cabin in the woods, where, once he got home, he planned to sleep all day into the evening. The early morning colors in the sky had burned off into a cool vibrant blue with not a cloud to be seen. The newly paved road sloped along through the mountains like a snake, the drive smooth and one that he should have enjoyed as he did his routine back and forth from the cabin to town and back again.

But the spot where he'd pulled over was different.

Castle gripped the steering wheel so hard his knuckles turned white. This was the place he had been too scared to stop at time and time again, a place where he'd normally step harder on the gas pedal if only to get past it faster.

This was where David had died.

And that morning as Castle sat, fighting back tears as he stared down the gully toward the woods, he saw a figure standing at the edge of the trees, staring at him expectantly. He wore the same black leather jacket, the same stuffed and grass-stained jeans, the same tawny leather boots as what David had been wearing when he had crashed.

David waved.

Castle choked back a sob and made himself wave back.

Thank you for reading

Hallowed Oblivion

If you felt moved by the story, I'd love for you to leave an honest review of your feelings. Reviews can be left on Goodreads, Bookbub, TikTok, Twitter, Insta, Facebook, etc. I appreciate you taking a chance on me and my work. As an indie/self-pub author, it means the world.

Thank you and Happy Halloween (all year long)!

ABOUT THE AUTHOR

PHOTO CREDIT: © COLIN BOROWSKE 2022

Katherine Silva is a Maine author of dark fiction, a connoisseur of coffee, and victim of cat shenanigans. She is a two-time Maine Literary Award finalist for speculative fiction and a member of the Horror Writers of Maine, The Horror Writers Association, and New England Horror Writers Association. Katherine is also a founder of Strange Wilds Press and Dark Taiga Creative Writing Consultations. Her latest works, ORCHARDS and HALLOWED OBLIVION, are short stories within THE WILD DARK universe and are now available wherever books are sold.